BADIR AND THE BEAVER

BADIR AND THE BEAVER

Shannon Stewart

Illustrated by
Sabrina Gendron

orca Echoes

ORCA BOOK PUBLISHERS

Library and Archives Canada Cataloguing in Publication

Stewart, Shannon, 1966–, author
Badir and the beaver / Shannon Stewart, author; Sabrina Gendron, illustrator.
(Orca echoes)

Issued in print and electronic formats.
ISBN 978-1-4598-1727-2 (softcover). — ISBN 978-1-4598-1728-9 (PDF). —
ISBN 978-1-4598-1729-6 (EPUB)

I. Gendron, Sabrina, 1984–, illustrator II. Title.
PS8587.T4894B33 2019   jc813'.54   C2018-904687-2
C2018-904688-0

Simultaneously published in Canada and the United States in 2019
Library of Congress Control Number: 2018954098

Summary: In this illustrated early chapter book, new Canadian Badir
confuses the beaver in his neighborhood park for a very large rat.

Orca Book Publishers gratefully acknowledges the support for its publishing
programs provided by the following agencies: the Government of Canada,
the Canada Council for the Arts and the Province of British Columbia through
the BC Arts Council and the Book Publishing Tax Credit.

Cover artwork and interior illustrations by Sabrina Gendron
Edited by Liz Kemp
Author photo by Michael Diner

ORCA BOOK PUBLISHERS
orcabook.com

Printed and bound in Canada.

22 21 20 19 • 4 3 2 1

With thanks to my generous students at the Conseil scolaire francophone. And special thanks to Kirsten Pendreigh and Faziah Gamaz for their guidance.

Chapter
ONE

"It was a giant rat!" Badir said, spreading his hands wide apart.

"Rats are not that big," Nate said. "They're only this big." He held his hands closer together to show Badir the size of a rat in Canada.

"I saw him! He was swimming in the small lake near my home," insisted Badir.

"A lake? We live in the city, Badir. There is no lake around here."

"A little lake," Badir tried to explain, spreading his arms out again.

"Right," said Nate. "You saw a rat the size of a poodle in a little lake. Now I've heard everything!"

Badir sighed. No one believed him. But the previous night he had seen the rat swimming in the water. He'd been taking a walk with his mother in Hinge Park. His mother had sat on a bench with the twins while Badir explored the paths around the park. There were songbirds in the trees and flowers blooming in the gardens.

Badir had just walked over a bridge when he heard the rustling of leaves and saw some bushes shaking back and forth. He walked farther along the path, and when he rounded the bend, he saw it.

A giant rat was swimming in the water with a stick in its mouth! It had

dark-brown fur, a little black nose and small ears flattened against the side of its head. The rat was a really good swimmer. Badir ran back to get his mother.

"I don't see it, Badir," she said, after she followed him over the bridge. They looked and looked, but the rat had disappeared.

"It was huge!" Badir said.

"I'm sure it was," she said.

* * *

After recess there was math. Badir was good with numbers.

"Numbers are so easy!" Badir said.

Marlene sighed. "You shouldn't brag."

"Brag? What does *brag* mean?" asked Badir.

"When you're good at something and you let everyone know about it," Marlene said, rolling her eyes.

"But I *am* good at numbers!" said Badir. He took out his pencil and started writing down the answers to the addition problems. "My brain is like a calculator. I can add these numbers in my head."

Mr. George, the teacher, stood beside Badir and watched him write down his answers.

"You are very good with numbers," he said, putting check marks beside all of Badir's answers.

"See?" Badir said, looking over at Marlene. "I'm not bragging."

Mr. George laughed.

Nate put his hand in the air.

"Yes, Nate?" Mr. George said.

"I think Badir likes to exaggerate things."

"What do you mean?" asked Mr. George.

"He said he saw a rat that was this big!" Nate spread his arms wide. Some of the other children in the class giggled.

"No! said Badir. "It was this big!" He held his hands out so Mr. George could see exactly how big the rat was.

"Really?" said Mr. George, smiling.

"It was swimming across the lake in the park."

"Do you mean Hinge Park?" said Mr. George. "It's a pond, not a lake, Badir. But I've seen rats there too. And squirrels and raccoons."

"See!" said Badir, jumping up in his seat. "Mr. George sees rats too!"

"Well, not ones that big," said Mr. George. "But I guess I'll have to keep my eyes open! Maybe you saw a dog swimming?"

"NO!" yelled Badir. "It was a rat!"

"Okay, okay," said Mr. George. "Let us know if you see it again."

After school Badir waited for his brother, Anis, to walk him home. Anis was in high school, and he was often tired and grumpy when he met Badir. Anis found it difficult to study in English all day long.

The boys walked by a travel agency on Main Street. Anis stopped. In the window there was a travel poster showing palm trees, clear blue water, a sandy beach and a white hotel. There were children playing on the sand.

"I miss home," said Anis, looking at the poster. Badir knew Anis also missed his friends. They used to spend every afternoon after school playing soccer in the fields near their home in Tunisia.

"We may have had beautiful, warm seas at home," said Badir, "but we didn't have giant rats who are very good swimmers!"

Anis looked at his little brother. "Enough about the huge rat, Badir! No one believes you!"

Badir smiled.

"One day you will believe me," he said. "I saw what I saw."

Chapter
TWO

When Badir and Anis came home, there were chores to do. Then Badir played with the twins while his mother rested in the bedroom. Anis sat at the kitchen table, doing his homework.

Badir unlocked the baby gate that kept the twins out of the kitchen. He took some tins of beans out of a cupboard.

He built a tower of beans in the living room.

The twins knocked it down.

He lined up the tins on the floor.

The twins drummed on them with wooden spoons.

He rolled the tins toward each twin, bumping their feet.

The twins squealed with joy when the beans knocked their toes.

Badir's mother woke up from her nap. Anis frowned as he tried to study his English.

"No more beans," Badir told the twins. "You're too noisy."

"*Salaam*!" said their father, unlocking the front door. He held grocery bags in his arms. The boys helped him unload the lettuce, tomatoes, lentils and milk in the kitchen.

Badir knew his brother was very hungry. Anis was watching his mother as she started to make dinner.

It was Ramadan, and Badir's family was fasting for the month. They could not eat any food from sunrise to sundown. Badir was too young to fast for the whole day, but he still had to remember not to lose his temper or say angry words. Ramadan was a time for good deeds, a time when it was especially important to be kind and help others.

The twins started to cry, pointing to the cans of beans.

"Take the twins for a walk," said his mother. "We will eat and pray when the sun goes down."

Badir and Anis buckled the twins into their double stroller.

"Let's go to the park," said Badir. "Maybe we'll see the giant rat."

Badir pushed the Down button on the elevator. When it stopped and the doors opened, there was a girl with spiky black hair inside. She wore a baggy gray T-shirt that hung down to her knees. Someone had written *Too Tired, Don't Talk to Me* across the front of the shirt with a black felt-tip pen. Beside the girl was a large, hairy dog.

"Salaam!" said Badir.

The girl just looked at him.

"Salaam means 'hello,'" Badir said.

"Oh," said the girl.

"What is your dog's name?"

"Oscar," said the girl, giving the leather leash a little tug.

"I'm Badir, and this is my brother Anis."

The girl ignored him. Anis watched the numbers light up above the elevator door.

When the doors opened, the girl turned around. "You're new here, right?" she asked Badir.

"Yes."

"I can tell," she said, pulling her dog's leash and walking away.

"Do you have to talk to everyone you meet?" asked Anis.

"I just wanted to be friendly," said Badir.

"I've seen that girl in my high school. Not everyone is as friendly as you."

* * *

When they arrived at the park, Badir rushed ahead to the pond. But there was no rat in the water. Anis pushed the stroller across the bridge and stood beside Badir.

"It's almost sunset," said Anis. "Forget about the rat." He unbelted one of the twins and began to rock him in his arms.

"Look!" Badir cried, pointing to the shore. Some of the bushes were shaking back and forth. "Over there!"

Chapter
THREE

Anis's eyes opened wide. A large animal was waddling out of the bushes, a small branch in its mouth. It walked into the water and floated into the middle of the pond.

"I told you it was a rat!" said Badir. "The biggest rat in the world!"

"That's not a rat!" said a woman in a bright-red jacket who had stopped to look over the railing with the boys.

She reached into her pocket and pulled out a handful of coins. She plucked out a nickel and gave it to Badir.

"This is a beaver," she said, tapping the image on the silver coin. "And so is that." She pointed to the animal in the pond.

Badir looked at the coin in the palm of his hand. Then he studied the rat, which had the same strange wide tail shaped like a short paddle.

"They are the same!" He smiled at the woman. "We don't have this kind of animal in Tunisia, where I used to live."

"Then you probably didn't have beaver lodges either." The woman laughed and pointed across the pond. A large dome made out of branches rose from the shore.

"That beaver is quite the builder, isn't he?" she said. "He wove all those

branches together with mud. He sleeps there during the day and comes out to find food at dusk."

"This beaver eats his meals after sunset, just like us during Ramadan!" Badir said.

The woman chuckled and walked away. She called over her shoulder, "Welcome to Canada! That beaver is our national symbol!"

Badir and Anis admired the beaver lodge. It was a fine home. Badir was amazed the beaver could make such a sturdy home out of sticks and mud.

"Look, Badir!" said Anis.

The beaver had climbed to the edge of the pond and was nibbling on a branch. He held it carefully between his front feet and used them skillfully, like two small hands.

"We had better hurry home," said Anis, looking at the sky.

As they pushed the twins home, they saw the girl from the elevator walking along the street with her dog. She scowled and crossed to the other side when she saw them.

"What did we do to her?" asked Badir.

"Some people are better off left alone," said Anis.

Chapter
FOUR

In the living room of their apartment, Badir and his family listened to the sound of the prayer call on their wall clock. Then they each drank a glass of milk and ate some sweet dates to break their fast before praying. After prayers they sat down to eat *iftar*, the meal at the end of the day. Tonight Badir's mother had made delicious lentil soup, *tajine* stew and salad.

Badir's father looked tired. He worked at a car-detailing shop where he spent all day vacuuming people's cars and washing them inside and out. He had owned a grocery store in Tunisia. Badir and Anis had always stopped in for a samosa on their way home from school. His father knew most of his customers by name and often asked them about their families and their work. At the car-detailing shop, he knew no one.

Badir watched his family sip their lentil soup slowly. He had eaten lunch at school, but this soup was the first food Anis and his parents had eaten since sunrise. They had not even had a sip of water during the day.

"You must be so hungry," said Badir.

His father nodded. "It takes discipline to eat slowly when we are fasting all day long. But then, many people in this world go hungry every day. And they don't have an iftar dinner. We are lucky, Badir. Remember that."

Badir took the nickel out of his pocket. He explained how he and Anis had seen the giant rat and that it was really a beaver.

"This is the national symbol of Canada?" said his father, looking at the beaver on the coin. "I wonder why."

***

Before Badir went to bed, he sat at the computer to write an email to his teacher.

Deer Mr. George,

This is Badir. You told me to tell you if I saw rat again and I did. But it is not rat. It is a beaver who eats at night. Just like my family at Ramadan. Now you can beleeve me.

Good nite.

Chapter
FIVE

Very early the next morning, before the sun had climbed into the sky, Badir's family got up to make *suhoor,* the breakfast meal for Ramadan. On the table they placed eggs, cheese, fruit, pita bread and *fattoush*, a salad made of vegetables.

Badir's family ate well. Their suhoor would be the last food they would enjoy before iftar, the evening meal, many

27

hours later. After breakfast Badir and Anis went to mosque with their father to recite their dawn prayers. Afterward, Anis walked Badir to school through streets busy with morning traffic.

At school, Mr. George smiled when he saw Badir. "Would you like to tell the class about your news?" he asked.

Badir nodded and cleared his throat. "I did not see a rat in the park. Instead, I saw a beaver. Which is also on this coin."

He held his nickel up for the class to see. "My beaver lives in a lodge, and he eats at night, just like my family during Ramadan."

Badir looked over at Nate.

"And he *is* this big," said Badir, spreading his hands out. "I did not exaggerate."

"Thank you, Badir," said Mr. George. "I'm surprised to hear there's a beaver in Hinge Park, right in the middle of the city! But then again, beavers lived in our streams and ponds before there were even cities."

"What happened to them?" asked Nate.

"They were hunted almost into extinction," said Mr. George.

"Why would anyone hunt a beaver?" Marlene asked.

"For their pelts," explained Mr. George. "Hundreds of years ago, Europeans wanted to wear coats and hats made from beaver fur. The underfur is very soft and waterproof. So beavers were hunted until there weren't very many left."

"That's a lot of fur hats!" Badir exclaimed.

"Yes!" Mr. George said, laughing. "But as the fur trade grew, so did Canada. Our early woodsmen canoed and portaged farther and farther inland to find more beavers. So the fur trade helped create our country. That's why the beaver is our national symbol."

"Will anyone try to hunt my beaver in the park?" Badir was worried.

"I don't think so," said Mr. George. "The city doesn't allow hunting."

Badir thought of the beaver in his pond in the middle of the city. Did he have enough food to eat? Was he safe inside his lodge? Badir knew what it was like to make a new home in a strange place.

"Don't worry about your beaver," said Mr. George. "Beavers are smart. They build lodges, cut down trees and create canals and dams, and they eat all kinds of bark and plants. Your city beaver knows how to look after himself."

"What if he's lonely?" asked Badir.

"He probably won't be." Mr. George laughed. "Beavers like to make families. They are monogamous, meaning they have the same partner for life. And they raise their kits, or baby beavers, until they are two years old. I bet your beaver will have his hands full soon enough."

Chapter
SIX

Anis met Badir after school. They walked down Main Street together, but before going home, Badir wanted to stop in the park to see if the beaver was awake.

The boys stood at the railing of the bridge by the pond and looked into the water. They saw two geese and their seven goslings. And they saw a seagull perched on a birdhouse sticking out of the water. But no beaver.

"He must be in his home," said Badir, pointing to the lodge.

"It's not a home—it's a mess!" said an angry voice behind them.

Badir and Anis turned around to see a tall man wearing rubber boots hammering a sign into the ground.

It read:

BEAVERS BEGONE

PARK TREES ARE
DISAPPEARING!

SIGN HERE IF YOU
WANT THIS
PEST GONE

"Why do you call him a *pest?*" Anis asked the man.

The man pointed to a broken tree near the pond. It looked like it had been stuck into a giant pencil sharpener.

"Look!" he said. "The beaver did this! The beaver is eating the park trees and then using the logs to make his lodge."

They looked, and it was true. An animal with strong teeth had chewed the tree trunk. All that was left was a gnawed stump.

"Beavers eat everything they can get their mouths around," said the man. "Bushes, saplings, trees. Nothing is safe. With a beaver in this pond, soon we won't have any park left!"

"It's a big park," said Badir. "There must be room for a little beaver."

The man looked at Badir. He looked him up. He looked him down.

"What do you know about beavers?" he asked.

"I know a lot about beavers," said Badir. "I know they are monogamous, and they take very good care of their children."

The man scowled. "Sorry, kid, but beavers do not belong in city parks. I plan on trapping this beaver and moving him somewhere else."

"Trapping him!" Badir imagined a metal cage snapping shut on his beaver.

"This beaver chose this park for his home. You can't just get rid of him!"

"Of course we can," said the man. "And you should stay out of it! You're too young to understand the problems a beaver brings to a city park."

The man squelched away in his rubber boots, holding his clipboard, off to get more people to sign their names to his petition.

Badir couldn't believe it. The man was going to trap the beaver, just like what Mr. George said had happened during the fur trade.

A woman walked up to the sign, holding her small white dog in her arms. "What a good idea!" she said and stooped to sign her name on the paper.

"Why are you signing this?" asked Badir.

"Because I'm afraid to walk Snowball in the park."

"Why?" asked Badir.

"*Why*?! She might get eaten by the beaver, of course!"

Badir laughed. "No, that's impossible! Beavers don't eat animals. They're herbivores! They eat grass and bark and pond weeds."

"Have you seen this beaver?" cried the woman. "He's a large, vicious rodent!" Snowball squirmed in her arms as she hugged her tightly.

"I think the kid knows more about beavers than you do," said a voice behind them. Everyone turned to see the girl from the elevator standing by the BEAVERS BEGONE sign. She was holding Oscar on a leash and wearing a new T-shirt that said, *Don't grow up. It's a trap!*

"Beavers are rodents," she said. "But they are not vicious. They like to chew, not bite."

The woman looked at the girl and snorted. Snowball growled and bared her teeth. Oscar panted loudly. He rolled over on the ground and stuck his paws up in the air.

"I think your little dog might be more vicious than a beaver," said the girl.

"She most certainly is not!" said the woman, squeezing Snowball to her chest. She turned and walked away. Snowball yapped at them over her shoulder.

Badir smiled at the girl. "Thank you," he said.

The girl nodded at the boys. She stared at the BEAVERS BEGONE sign.

"Looks like this beaver is in big trouble," she said.

"I know," said Badir. "We have to help him."

"Well," said the girl. "For starters, we could change the sign."

She reached into her back pocket and pulled out a big felt-tip pen.

"There!" she said, standing back to admire her work.

The sign now read:

BEAVERS BELONG

Badir and Anis smiled.

"That's better!" said Anis.

"Look!" said Badir. The tall man was coming back. He looked angry.

"What are you kids doing?!" he shouted.

"Run!" said the girl. The three of them ran out of the park as fast as they could go.

BEAVERS BEGONE

PARK TREES ARE
DISAPPEARING!

SIGN HERE IF YOU
WANT THIS
PEST GONE

Then, walking back to their apartment building, the girl told them her name was Rita.

"I've seen you at school," said Anis.

Rita let Badir hold Oscar's leash. Oscar pulled Badir the whole way home.

"Who's walking whom?" asked a police officer at the intersection.

Badir looked back and saw Anis and Rita talking. Anis was pointing to the poster on the travel agency's window. Rita looked interested in what he was saying.

Anis has found a friend, thought Badir.

Oscar peed on a fire hydrant and then pulled him into their building.

Chapter
SEVEN

That evening Rita came over to share their Ramadan meal. Anis had asked his father if it was okay to bring a guest to iftar.

"Of course," he said. "Friends are always welcome."

Badir's father laughed when he saw Rita's T-shirt.

"I agree 100 percent!" he said. "Growing up *is* a trap!"

They drank glasses of milk, ate dates and then had their iftar dinner of lamb and rice. Badir told his parents about the petition to get rid of the beaver in the park. He told them about the ruined tree and the man with rubber boots.

Badir's mother nodded thoughtfully. "It is a small park for a beaver," she said.

"But a large-enough park for a man with a petition," said Badir's father.

Rita was quiet during dinner, but she finished everything on her plate.

"Does your mother cook lamb?" asked Badir's mother.

"I live with my father," said Rita. "He works until late, so this is nice. I don't usually eat with anyone," she added.

"We are happy to share with you," said Badir's mother.

For dessert, Badir's father had made his famous lemon pie with pistachios.

Rita ate it slowly and carefully, licking her spoon after each bite.

"This is so much better than instant noodles and broccoli," she said. "Thank you."

Before Badir and his family went to mosque, Rita's father knocked on their door. Rita had left a note telling him she had been invited to dinner. Badir's father gave him a leftover piece of pie.

"Can I go to Rita's apartment?" asked Badir. "We need to make signs for the park, to tell people the truth about the beaver."

His parents looked at each other. Usually they went together as a family to mosque.

"Helping the beaver is a good deed!" Badir said.

"It's okay with me," said Rita's father.

"Okay," said Badir's mother. "That beaver is lucky to have you. Anis will come and get you after mosque."

* * *

Oscar was waiting at the door of Rita's apartment. He slobbered over Badir's leg when he came in. Badir heard a scrabbling sound in the corner of the living room. He looked over and saw a cage. A soft white rabbit stared out at him.

"What's its name?" he asked.

"White Rabbit," said Rita. She tossed markers and pieces of cardboard to Badir.

"Let's get busy," she said. "If people learn about the beaver, they'll start to care about him. We can put the signs up in the park tomorrow after school."

Badir worked on a sign with Rita. They wrote, *Beaver at work. Leave him alone!* "You're really good at printing," said Badir.

"I have had lots of practice," said Rita, pointing to a pile of T-shirts on a chair. Each one had a different slogan written on it.

Nope. Not today.

*I'd rather be hanging out
with my rabbit.*

*I always YAWN when I'm paying
attention.*

Badir thought about the beaver's amazing lodge. He wrote, *Beavers are people too!* on his own sign.

"Beavers aren't people," Rita said.

"They are like little people," explained Badir. "They build dams and ponds and canals. So do we. They can cut down trees. So can we. Their beaver lodge has a front door, a mudroom and a bedroom. Like ours. And in winter, if it's cold, steam comes out of the top of their lodge like smoke from a chimney. What other animal does that?"

"Cool," said Rita. "How do you know so much about beavers?"

"I've done my research," said Badir.

He walked over to White Rabbit's cage. She was chewing on some lettuce. Badir stuck his finger into the cage, and White Rabbit hopped over to sniff it. She licked his finger. Then she nibbled his finger. Then she bit his finger.

"Ouch!" said Badir, pulling away. The rabbit nibbled on the cage, eyeing him.

Badir stared at the cage. "Rita, what is this cage made from?"

"Chicken wire," said Rita.

"And this makes a good cage for rabbits?"

"She doesn't like to chew on the wire," explained Rita.

"Interesting," said Badir. "Very, very interesting. Maybe chicken wire can work with other animals too."

Rita smiled at Badir. "I think I know what you're thinking, Badir!"

When Anis came to pick him up, Badir told him they were going to put up signs in the park the next day.

* * *

Before bed, Badir sat down at the computer.

Deer Mr. George,
This is Badir. I need your help. The fur trade is happening again! A man wants to trap the park beaver becuz he is eating the park trees.

I have a plan! Maybe we can save the trees with chiken wire!

Good nite.

Anis read Badir's email before he sent it. "Chicken wire?" he asked. "Do you really think that will work?"

Badir shrugged. "I know what I know," he said.

"I don't think you know so much," said Anis.

"I know a lot of things," said Badir, getting into his pajamas.

"I know beavers' teeth never stop growing," said Badir. "That's why they can chew on trees. If you chewed on a tree, Anis, you wouldn't have any teeth left!"

Anis smiled as he got into his pajamas.

"And I know beavers have orange teeth! That is because they have iron in their teeth, which makes them very strong and sharp."

"Go to sleep, Badir," said Anis.

"And they have a second set of eyelids, like goggles, that let them see underwater."

Anis threw a pillow at Badir.

"And they are amazing engineers," said Badir dreamily. "No other animal can change the world like a beaver can..."

Badir fell asleep, dreaming of swimming underwater with a branch between his teeth. He was swimming toward his home.

Chapter
EIGHT

"He said he wanted to trap the beaver!" said Badir, showing his friends one of the signs he had made with Rita.

"That's terrible!" Nate gasped. "The beaver has a right to make his home in the park, doesn't he?"

"He does," said Mr. George. "And there's nowhere to relocate him to anyway. Other ponds and lakes have their own beavers. He needs his own space to raise a family."

"But there is no girl beaver."

"Female beaver," said Marlene.

"Not yet," said Mr. George. "But eventually our beaver friend will find a mate and have kits."

"With his beaver family, even more trees will be eaten!" Badir said.

Mr. George nodded. He drew a tree on the whiteboard with his marker, and a funny-looking beaver beside it.

"I think Badir is right. If we want to help our beaver, we need to protect the trees in the park. Does anyone have any ideas?"

Badir waved his arm in air. "I do! I do! I do!" he shouted.

But Mr. George asked Nate, who was sitting quietly with his hand raised.

"What about giving the beaver other trees from forests that have more trees?" suggested Nate.

Mr. George wrote on the board:

Solution 1: PROVIDE OTHER TREES

"That's a lot of work," said Samantha. "Someone would have to cut down the trees and bring them to Hinge Park."

"It's an interesting idea though," said Mr. George.

"Ask me! Ask me!" said Badir.

Mr. George did not seem to hear Badir.

"What about sprinkling something on the trees that beavers don't like to eat, like cayenne pepper?" suggested Marlene.

Mr. George wrote on the board:

Solution 2: CAYENNE PEPPER

"That could make the beaver sick," said Yayo.

"Mr. George! Mr. George!" Badir waved his hand again.

But Mr. George asked Max on the other side of the classroom.

"I was thinking we could wrap something around the trees, like blankets," said Max.

Mr. George wrote on the board:
Solution 3: BLANKET WRAP

"But a beaver could chew them up, couldn't they?" asked Amany.

"Still, it's an interesting idea," said Mr. George.

"What about spikes?" asked Isabelle. "We use them to stop pigeons from roosting on our roof."

"Spikes?" said Ryan. "That's mean!"

Mr. George wrote on the board:

Solution 4: SPIKES

"Oh! Oh! Oh!" said Badir.

Mr. George looked at Badir. "Okay, Badir. Your turn."

Badir gasped for air and rubbed his stretched-out shoulder.

"Chicken wire!" he shouted. "We can put chicken wire on the trees!"

Mr. George wrote on the board:

Solution 5: CHICKEN WIRE

He pointed to the board. "Five solutions," he said. "Let's see if we can make one work."

"I think all these ideas are good," said Jasminder, a quiet student who sat in the corner of the classroom. "But some of them are better than others. And if we combine our ideas, maybe we can find the best way to help the beaver."

Everyone stared at the five possible solutions.

"We could wrap chicken wire around the trees like a blanket," said Max.

"That would work," said Nate. "But would chicken wire stop a beaver?"

"Beavers have very sharp teeth," said Badir. "But chicken wire is made from metal. I don't think a beaver would want to chew on metal."

"I think it could work," said Mr. George. "Wrapping trees in chicken wire could protect them."

"But where would we get chicken wire?" asked Nate.

"I have some!" Marlene said. "We were just using rolls of it to puppy-proof

our garden. We still have some in our backyard."

"We have to hurry," said Badir. "The man was asking people to write their names down. If too many people want the beaver gone…" Badir couldn't finish his sentence. The class fell silent.

"It's very difficult to leave your home," Badir said. And then he put his head down on his desk.

"Don't worry, Badir," said Nate. "We'll help your beaver."

* * *

That afternoon Mr. George gave the class time to make some more beaver signs.

"If you are going to wrap trees in chicken wire, you had better let people know what you are doing," he said.

As the rest of the class made signs, Badir and Marlene used Mr. George's computer to do some research. Badir learned that beaver-destroyed trees could become bushier trees the following year, as new branches grew out from the stumps. Those branches became new places for birds to sing and perch. Marlene found out that beaver dams worked like giant water filters, keeping the waterways clean and healthy.

"Beavers are what you call a keystone species," Mr. George said. "Having beavers around makes it possible for other species to live there too."

"My beaver is the best," Badir stated. He smiled at Marlene.

"And that's not bragging. That's the truth!"

Chapter
NINE

After school Badir and Nate and Marlene waited at the front of the school for Anis. Badir grinned when he saw that Anis was walking with Rita. She was wearing a bright-purple T-shirt that said *Not a people person.* She was carrying the signs they had made the night before.

"This is my brother, Anis," said Badir. "And this is Rita. They go to the same high school."

"Ramadan *mubarak*!" said Nate and Marlene. Badir had taught them how to say "Happy Ramadan!" in Arabic.

Anis smiled. Rita pointed to Nate's backpack, which was full of sticks and poster paper. "What are those?" she asked.

"More signs!" said Badir. "Mr. George wants us to make sure people in the park know what we are doing."

Rita unrolled one of the signs:

SAVE A BEAVER

WRAP A TREE

"Cool," she said. Together they walked down Main Street and stopped at Marlene's house for the chicken wire. Marlene's mom gave them some gloves, a pair of pliers and a bag of cookies.

Rita frowned when she saw the chicken wire. "That's not a lot of wire," she said.

"It's a start," said Badir.

Rita handed her signs to Anis. "I have to get home and walk Oscar," she explained. "I'll meet you at the park later."

* * *

"Here is the lodge!" said Badir when they arrived at Hinge Park. They stood at the bridge railing, across from the beaver lodge. The beaver had been busy. More sticks and mud had been gathered to make his home even larger.

"He is such a good builder!" exclaimed Badir.

Marlene and Nate were impressed. The beaver had used lots of fresh mud to hold the sticks of his home in place.

"Check out the hockey stick," said Nate. Sticking out of the middle of the beaver lodge was a blue hockey stick.

"He's a recycling beaver!" said Marlene.

Anis and Badir walked over to the sign the man had hammered into the ground.

"Oh no!" said Badir. "Look!" Thirteen names were written on the petition. That meant thirteen people wanted to get rid of the beaver.

The tall angry man who had put up the sign was walking toward them in his rubber boots. He was still carrying his clipboard.

"So have you come to your senses?" he asked the boys. "There are lots of people who agree with me." He held his clipboard up so they could see an entire column of signed names.

Badir dug into his pocket and showed the man his nickel. The silver beaver glowed in the sun.

Badir pointed to the lodge.

"This beaver belongs here. He is busy making his home, and he will have a family someday. He needs some trees to chew to make his home, but we can protect the bigger trees."

The man stared at Badir. "How do you plan on doing that?" he asked.

Marlene sprang into action. She unrolled the chicken wire and wrapped it around a mature willow tree that stood near the edge of the stream. She made sure the wire went all the way to the base of the tree, so the beaver couldn't go under it.

She made sure the wire went high enough up the tree, so the beaver could not climb over it. She wrapped the chicken wire loosely around the trunk, so the tree wouldn't grow into it and injure its trunk. She showed everyone how to wrap the ends of the wire together with a pair of pliers so the mesh wouldn't unravel.

Everyone was impressed.

"You're a chicken-wire expert!" said Badir.

"My mom and dad both work in construction," she explained. "It comes naturally."

The man stepped back and looked at the tree.

"That's only one tree," he said. "What about all the other trees in the park?"

Badir and Anis and their friends looked up from the willow tree. It was true.

There were many trees a beaver could chew on, and they only had enough chicken wire for the one tree.

Chapter
TEN

"Well, it was worth a try," said the man, looking at the unhappy faces around him.

"We won't give up yet," said Badir.

Anis pointed at the bridge. "Look!"

Rita was walking across the bridge, carrying a huge armload of chicken wire. Oscar had a roll of chicken wire carefully strapped to his back.

Rita dropped her bundle on the ground.

Badir grinned.

"Piggy-bank savings come in handy," Rita said. "I figured you could use some more wire. I bought it at the hardware store."

"And my dad pitched in for some gloves and pliers," she said, pulling them out of a bag and passing them around.

She looked over at Badir, who had a huge grin on his face. "Well, don't just stand there! Let's get busy!"

And everyone got busy. As busy as beavers. They walked along the edge of the waterway, wrapping the trunks of the bigger trees in chicken wire. They made sure it was low enough, high enough and loose enough, just like Marlene had shown them.

As they worked, and the sun began to sink in the sky, Badir told his friends some interesting facts he had learned about beavers.

Did they know that beavers covered the branches and mud in their lodges with musk oil to mark their territory?

Did they know that beavers could spend fifteen minutes underwater without coming up for air?

Did they know that beavers slapped their tails on the water to alert other beavers about dangers?

"Enough about beavers, Badir," groaned Anis. "Let's get this work done."

Badir moved downstream and found a large tree that was difficult to reach, jutting out over the water. He wasn't sure he wanted to wade out into the water with his running shoes on. He was about to turn back when he saw a pair of rubber boots squelching along the shoreline. The tall man stood above him. He didn't look so angry anymore.

"Looks like you could use some help," he said.

Badir nodded and pointed to his sneakers. "They're new," he said.

The man pointed to his boots. "They're old," he said.

The man stood in the water and helped Badir wrap the tree in chicken wire.

"I've been thinking," said the man. "This is a pretty good idea you had for protecting the trees in the park."

"Thank you," said Badir, smiling. "This way, the beaver keeps his home and we also get to keep our park."

"You know, sharing the park with a beaver might not be as difficult as I thought," the man said. He pulled a

piece of paper out of his pocket. It was the petition with the signatures of people who wanted the beaver relocated.

He tore the paper into a bunch of little pieces and put the pieces back in his pocket. Then he held out his hand to Badir.

"My name is Geoffrey," he said.

"Salaam, Geoffrey!" said Badir, shaking his hand. "Anyone who is a friend of the beaver is a friend of mine!"

Chapter
ELEVEN

By the time the sun was low in the sky, many of the larger trees of Hinge Park were wrapped in chicken wire. A few smaller trees were left for the beaver to use as he needed. Badir and his friends had placed signs throughout the park, telling people about their beaver and how it was important for him to live in their park in the middle of the city, surrounded by apartments, traffic and people.

One sign read:

BIODIVERSITY MEANS
BEAVERS IN OUR BACKYARD!

Geoffrey was impressed.

"I guess this park *is* biodiverse," he said. "Since we've been wrapping trees, I've seen a family of geese, ducks, a rat, two squirrels, all sorts of insects, all kinds of songbirds…"

"And I've seen raccoons and skunks here before," said Rita.

"Look!" said Anis, pointing to the stream.

There was a small, sleek head swimming along the waterway.

"Our beaver!" shouted Badir, running to the railing.

The beaver was swimming through the water, his large, flat tail guiding him like a rudder through the water. Below the group of curious faces, he lumbered onto the shoreline and disappeared into some bulrushes growing beside the pond.

"Wow!" said Marlene and Nate. "He's amazing!"

They waited for a few minutes. They could hear a gnawing sound, and they saw the tops of some bushes shaking.

The grasses rustled, and out came the beaver, with a leafy branch in his mouth.

"Did you know," said Badir, "that a beaver's lips close behind his teeth, so he can carry sticks without getting water in his mouth?"

Everyone watched as the beaver slipped into the pond and began to swim back to his lodge, dragging the branch through the water beside him. Just before the lodge, the beaver dove and disappeared.

"How does he get into his home?" Marlene asked.

Everyone looked at Badir.

But it was Anis who answered.

"A beaver lodge has two underwater tunnels," he said. "They lead from the pond to inside the lodge so the beaver can make a quick escape from predators if he needs to."

Badir smiled. "How did you know that, Anis?"

Anis looked sheepish, and then he laughed.

"I guess I've been doing my own research," he said. "You're right, Badir. Beavers are fascinating."

"Listen!" said Rita.

They could hear the sound of gnawing and chewing inside the lodge.

After a couple of minutes, the beaver swam out of his lodge again. And then another beaver swam out of the lodge.

"It looks like our beaver friend has found a partner," said Geoffrey, smiling.

"Two beavers!" shouted Badir. "Then we have done a good deed. Our beaver's home is safe!"

Anis looked up at the sunset-pink sky. "Badir, we have to get home for iftar."

The brothers had started to say goodbye to their friends when they saw their family crossing the bridge.

Chapter
TWELVE

"There you are!" said their mother, holding out her arms.

"How did you know we were in the park?" asked Badir.

"How did we know?" asked his father, laughing. "Badir, all you've been talking about for the last week is this beaver!"

"And Rita told us about the chicken-wire work party," said their mother.

"So we thought you might like to invite your friends home for a Ramadan meal."

"Great idea!" said Badir.

"I would be honored," said Geoffrey. He told Badir's parents that the children were very good stewards of the park.

"Thanks to them, the beavers and trees can live together."

Nate and Marlene called their parents to ask if they could stay for dinner.

"I'm allowed!" each of them said.

"Are your parents making lamb again?" asked Rita, licking her lips.

"Lamb shish kebab and beet salad," said Anis. "My favorites!"

"Ramadan mubarak!" said Nate to the twins, as they all started to walk back to Badir's home.

Oscar began to bark loudly. He strained on his leash.

"Quiet, Oscar!" said Rita, but it was too late. Oscar had pulled away from her and was running back toward the pond, with his leash trailing on the ground.

"I'll get him!" said Badir, and he ran after Oscar.

"Come straight back!" yelled his father. "You have guests!"

"Right back!" shouted Badir over his shoulder. He knew Oscar liked to watch the ducks floating between the water plants. He followed Oscar's barking down the trail, and sure enough, he was barking at something in the water.

But it was not a duck.

It floated on the water beside the beaver lodge. It had a black head and white bands on its neck. Its back was also black and had white spots.

It was definitely not a rat.

It was certainly not a beaver.

And it was absolutely beautiful.

Badir reached into his pocket and took out a handful of coins.

He plucked out a one-dollar coin, a loonie, and stared at it. He looked at the creature on the water. And then he looked at the coin again. The bird gave a strange call. It was the strangest sound Badir had ever heard. It was half laugh and half cry.

Badir smiled.

He started to walk back home for dinner with Oscar on his leash.

I saw what I saw, he thought to himself. They just might believe me this time.

SHANNON STEWART teaches in a francophone school in Vancouver, British Columbia, where she has had the opportunity to meet and learn from students from all over the world. She is the author of *Sea Crow* (Orca, 2004), *Alphabad: An Alphabet Book for Wicked Children!* (Key Porter Books, 2005) and *Captain Jake* (Orca, 2008). She holds an MFA in creative writing from the University of British Columbia.

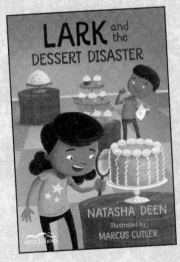